Jennifer Maksimovich

Two Shadows

A Ghost Story based upon Real Events

2021

Two Shadows
Written by Jennifer Maksimovich

Editor
Lisa Gilliam

Graphic Design
Denis Vikic

Two Shadows

To Baba Zorka:
A tea leaf reader, ghost story lover & teller,
coming up flights of stairs for my liver.
I'm forever thankful for your larger-than-life
personality and mothering presence!
Memory eternal.

Table of Contents

Chapter 1

THE DEVIL.

SAMANTHA'S EYES DARTED BACK AND FORTH in quick spasmatic movements. Her heart thumped in her ears as she held her breath in terror. "SSHHHH! Don't talk! I can feel it listening!"

Paula drew in her breath to hold it but felt like screaming. Had her friend truly gone mad? Or was it more sinister than that? She waited for what seemed like an eternity before she heard a muffled "Okay... okay... but I have to keep this short. I know you think I've completely lost it, but I'm telling you, it's real what I'm experiencing!" Samantha's voice trailed off, and a pregnant silence delivered itself to Paula's receptive ears.

"Sam, you just need to rest! You're exhausted. With all you've been through recently, I'm surprised you're even standing! Now if you want me to fly over, you know I'll jump on a plane tonight." Paula half hoped Sam wouldn't accept her offer. They had grown up together since the third grade and spent so much time together, they were almost able to finish each other's sentences.

Paula had lost touch with Samantha after they went to separate colleges and later got married, Paula moving to the East Coast while Samantha headed to Southern California. But like most strong female friendships, nothing could come between them. Neither time nor distance could breach that special bond.

Still, Paula was sheepishly relieved to hear her friend reply, "No, absolutely not! You have your mother to care for, and besides, I'm not sure whether this *thing* could attach itself to you. I don't want to take any chances. I just need someone to talk to, someone I can trust who won't commit me. Derek thinks I'm crazy enough already! He says it's just a menopausal hormone imbalance and nothing more!" Sam let out a disapproving snort.

Paula laughed. "Men! I swear the human race would be long gone if all we had to rely on were these dingdongs!" Paula waited for Sam's reaction but was met with silence. "Sam? Hello... Sam!" Paula could hear shallow breathing and a strange sound like static clicks coming through the phone and a weird buzzing sound, then nothing. The phone went dead.

Sam held on to her cell phone with so much pressure her knuckles turned white from the strain. As the skin lifted off the back of her neck like a cat hunching its back, she tried to remain calm, but there was no overriding millions of years of evolution. Her fight-or-flight response had kicked in, and Sam was being sucked into the biochemical feed-back of fear.

Was it really there, this shifting dark figure? *How could it exist in a well-lit room*? she thought as the lights began to flicker. Her own shadow cowered before the growing dark entity, and she was getting dizzy. Not sure how much time had passed, she awoke to her husband, Derek, shaking her and lightly tapping her face.

"Sam! Sam! There's my girl. What in the world happened?" Derek said as Sam started coming around.

Sam got up, shaking, with Derek's assistance, sank into their big sofa chair, and said, "That's the thing, it's not of this world!" She started sobbing uncontrollably. It took an hour for Derek to finally calm his wife down enough to get clues into what Sam had been experiencing this past month.

Sam recalled the first time she experienced the shadow presence, during a conference she attended in the Bay Area, staying at a historic hotel, the Fairmont, in the posh Knob Hill area in the heart of the city. The hotel had existed since 1907, built by two daughters, Theresa "Tessie" Fair Oelrichs and Virginia "Birdie" Fair Vanderbilt, who built the hotel in honor of their silver mining millionaire father (net worth of $50M in 1880), the Silver King, US Senator James Graham Fair. Their hotel was almost completed when the infamous 1906 San Francisco earthquake struck, and while the structure survived, the interior was damaged by fire, and the opening was delayed until the following year. The Fair sisters somewhat clairvoyantly sold their interest in the hotel just two weeks prior to the completion date of the hotel and the catastrophic earthquake that followed. Despite their fortuitous foresight, neither lived to see the Fairmont Hotel opening, as they both perished in the Great Quake. It is said that their spirits still caretake the hotel, along with its guests, as their good upbringing as hostesses would command. Another spirit that resides in the esteemed hotel is a prostitute that was murdered in one of the rooms. It is said that she sits in a red teddy, chatting up guests. And if those spirits weren't enough, the 7th floor of the hotel used to serve as an infirmary for soldiers during World War II, with several male spirits still roaming the halls there.

Of course at the time, Sam was privy to no such ghostly information. She noticed only how beautiful and expansive her room was, like a small home, and that everything was old yet restored to its original grandeur. But right from the beginning, after checking into her room, there were small things, like the feeling something was caught in her eye when she went to the bathroom to wash her face. It wasn't make-up or anything she could identify, but it felt like a speck was caught, which she couldn't blink away. And the lights flickered whenever she turned them on and periodically throughout the evening. The odd bumps, thumps, and clicks throughout the room, well, those could be explained away as hotel rooms, especially old ones, tend to "settle." But something truly unsettling happened the next day, when she was awoken to the drumming of fingers on top of the wooden frame of her bed.

Sam recalled waking up to that drumming sound, like an impatient staccato sound that fingers make when someone is waiting for time to pass. The drumming followed one another in sequence from pinky to pointer, 1-2-3-4, click, click, click, click, like galloping horses running in place right over her head. *What was that exactly?* Sam thought at the time, realizing it was morning before her alarm was to go off. The room was well lit with the breaking rays of sunshine, yet those fingers banged away until Sam got out of bed and started her day.

Sam was in too much of a rush to get to the first discussion at the conference to think much more of this odd wake-up call. But later that evening, more oddities in the room, more flickering lights, and something in her eye that she couldn't blink out. She heard tapping sounds throughout the room and felt pinprick sensations on her body at times. Sam felt that she wasn't alone in the room, that there was another presence there, watching her, trying to communicate with her with weird sounds she drowned out with the TV. By the third evening, she couldn't stand to be in that room and didn't sleep a wink, with all the lights on and the TV running. She felt such relief to check out of that hotel and fly home.

But that evening after unpacking and lying down in bed, thinking of sweet slumber, she felt something hit her face. She opened her eyes and looked down on the comforter at a piece of shag carpet from the floor. How did that get ripped up from the floor to be flicked in her face like an insult? This was meant to get her attention in the rudest way and was not something that could be easily brushed aside. Now it had her attention, and she wondered whether that thing from the Fairmont hotel room could have followed her home.

The next day, Sam woke up to the same sound of drumming fingers, this time on her own headboard. She jolted out of bed and looked around the headboard, but nothing could explain that sick joke but that entity having followed her home all the way back to San Diego!

Sam looked up the hotel online later that day, discovering that the Fairmont was one of the oldest hotels in San Francisco, that it survived the Big Quake and served as a hospital during World War II. Sam's investigation also yielded the Lady in Red, who was believed to be a mistress of the night. "Oh great! Why am I just now learning this, and why or how would some ungodly entity follow me of all people home?"

During the online research, Sam also found that signs of ghosts or poltergeists can be the feeling of sharp pinpricks throughout your body and the feeling of something being caught in a person's eyes, just like she experienced. But what was this exactly? The Lady in Red or something more sinister?

Derek laughed it off, saying Sam had an overactive imagination, or perhaps underactive hormones. It wasn't enough that Sam had to deal with being a middle-aged menopausal woman, but now she had to deal with harassment from both her husband and this unidentifiable "shadow." It was enough to make any sane woman feel like she was going mad.

Derek was a good man and faithful husband who loved his wife, but he just didn't believe in this nonsense when he heard Sam's story about the Fairmont and feeling the same eeriness whenever she went up-stairs to the bedroom. Derek racked it up to too many miles flown with very little rest and Sam suffering night sweats like she was burning up from the inside. But Sam was not sweating because of hormones anymore; she simply sweated like a Pavlovian response whenever she found herself alone in her own bedroom with that wicked presence.

When Sam would try to say her prayers in front of her home altar before sleeping, as she did every night before bed, flickering pinpricks would try to still her lips, like tiny rubber bands slapping her mouth as she tried to say the Lord's Prayer, or any prayers for that matter. This entity didn't want her to communicate with God, and once she lay down in bed, that was when the battle would start. She could feel this shadow presence trying to jump into her, occupy her body like a cloak, and Sam would pray and curse it to "Get out! This is *not* your home! You are *not* welcomed here!" saying the Jesus prayer over and over. "Oh Lord, Jesus Christ, the Son of God, have mercy upon me, a sinner!" while getting up, pacing the floor and spraying holy water throughout the room, onto herself and her husband sleeping in bed, much to his chagrin. The harassment would subside for a minute or two, and then it would come back, taunting her because she couldn't control it, nor did it care that it was an uninvited guest in Sam's home.

Sam had reached out to her friend Paula for comfort after a particularly brutal week of battling this apparition night after night. She started to think she was in fact going crazy, but the presence was too alive to deny, seeming to gain strength from feeding off Sam's fear. Now Sam was constantly terrorized in her own home, and this last apparition took all of Sam's resistance, temporarily snapping her out of consciousness.

Derek, consoling his wife, had never seen her so fragile mentally or physically. He was coming to the realization that this might not be all in Sam's head. He, too, had an unexplained feeling of being pounced upon in the night whenever Sam did battle with the entity, and it would tire of fighting her and try to jump onto Derek. He dared not admit it to Sam initially, trying to keep her calm and himself feeling in control. Yet there it was, this unseen shadow that somehow was invisible yet "felt" like something real, weighted, that could swap terrorizing one warm human body to another. Derek also couldn't deny having extremely strange dreams.

In one, he was sitting with Samantha in a fancy restaurant with a bar, and a woman was sitting across from them, only staring at Sam, but Sam wouldn't even look her way, never giving this woman the time of day. The bar and patrons were all from the 1920s, clothing like flappers, and Derek felt like he was in a movie when several mobster-looking men walked into the room, looking to shoot Derek and Sam. Derek grabbed Sam's arm and ran out of the bar, with the men in fast pursuit. They tried to duck down narrow alleyways to avoid these menacing figures trying to kill them, for what reason, Derek didn't know. When Derek awoke, he wanted to tell his wife what he dreamt, but decided not to fuel her growing panic and anxiety.

Derek hugged his wife tight. "I know you don't want to hear this, but let's try to go to bed. Both of us could use more rest right now."

Sam doubted she would ever sleep soundly again but tried to be brave, for at least her husband's sake, if not her own, as she couldn't show any weakness to the shadow. That night, besides the thumps and clicks in her ears under her pillow and pinpricks throughout her legs, it was unusually "quiet." But before both Derek and Sam rose the next morning, the entire bed shook them awake, not just a gentle to and fro shaking or even as an earthquake might shake an entire room side to side or up and down, but physically like a signal wave rolled through the bed, cresting and falling across the middle section of the mattress. No physics could explain or contort the bed in that way. This was when Derek finally admitted to Sam his strange dreams and feelings of being "jumped" during the night when Sam was able to toss off the shadow.

Now Sam had the ammunition she needed. It wasn't all in her head, she wasn't going crazy, this was some unexplainable and malevolent force that for some reason she alone didn't have the power to overcome, even with holy water, incessant praying, and demanding the shadow to depart to where it came from. Sage incense smoking all rooms, doorways, windows, nothing had worked. Sam swallowed her pride and called her Orthodox priest, Father Dushan Vukovich, asking him to help her expel the entity from her home. To her surprise, Father Dushan didn't seem judgmental of either her mental state or her experience, saying he had been asked this before and would be happy to help and would come by Tuesday afternoon.

Sam sat back down with a long sigh of relief; a huge weight lifted off her shoulders. She was physically and mentally at the end of her rope with the ominous harassments that seemed to escalate, and finally, not only was her sanity validated but she found the first hope for banishing this dark spirit.

When Father Dushan came to the home, he was dressed in a dark black robe, carrying a black leather "doc kit" satchel that looked like an old-fashioned doctor's bag. Sam and Derek greeted him with three kisses as is tradition, one for each cheek and a third to seal the greeting in Trinity. Father Dushan didn't waste time and set about to work, opening his large bag and pulling out a Bible, holy water and oil, a beeswax candle, a golden crucifix, and a censer on a chain with a cross on the top. Father Dushan proceeded to light the charcoal tabs to burn the incense in the censer until thick smoke emanated from it, smelling like frankincense and myrrh. He swung the censer, which made a melodic clanging with twelve bells hanging from the chains. He moved swiftly and gracefully about the rooms in the home, saying prayers in church Slavonic, a 2000-year-old language that knows no blasphemy, swear words, or sinful connotations. He read from a portion of his Bible that was specifically to exorcise any evil or demonic forces, and blessed both Sam and Derek, putting holy oil on their heads. It was in some ways such a simple act, nothing fancy or earth-shattering like you see in the movies, but so eloquently and quietly powerful.

After that point, everything stopped. The poltergeist's mischievous antics ceased, and Samantha and Derek's life went back to normal, with peaceful slumbering nights, something Sam didn't think was ever going to be possible again.

Yet Samantha was still left wondering what exactly the entity was that could be so powerful to tear carpet pieces up, flow through their bed, making it feel like waves on the ocean, and sinisterly disturb her and even her husband's peace of mind. And why wasn't she strong enough to rid it herself? Was there something inherently wrong with her, or was she weak? What drew this entity to her?

Chapter 2

THE MOON.

EVENTUALLY EVEN THESE QUESTIONS SUBSIDED. Paula, of course, got wind of everything and invited her friend to come visit her just to get away from it all. Samantha was happy to oblige and was able to get cheap airfare out of San Diego to Mystic, CT, where Paula resided with her mother, Jackie, and their dog, Barkly.

When Sam's plane landed at Providence Airport, she couldn't wait to see her friend and reminisce about old times. Paula's father and mother had retired to Mystic, and when Paula's father had passed several years prior, her mother had fallen into depression, and then Jackie's subsequent battle with cancer brought Paula to the small, quaint New England community along the sea to care for her ailing mother.

Paula gave her friend a huge hug, grabbed her big black Louis Vuitton suitcase, and while hoisting it into the back of the Subaru, joked, "I said come for a visit, not move in!"

Sam laughed. "Well, it's just my 'default' bag I bring to every business trip, so it's already semi-packed and ready to go, so less work than pulling it all out into another bag."

As they drove along, the ladies chatted about the state of their lives and reminisced about old times. Paula was careful not to touch on the topic of that shadow presence that put her friend into such a state of mania and despair. She knew there would be a time for this after easing into the slower vibe of life in Mystic.

When they arrived, it was getting dark, and as Sam pulled her luggage out of the back of the car, a large black dog came running out of the alley, snarling and growling, heading straight for Sam. Shocked, Sam quickly blocked the dog from lunging at her with her large hard-sided suitcase. The menacing dog circled to try to attack from behind, and again Sam blocked the dog with her case. The rabid dog was totally intent on Sam, trying once more, then coming up against the blocking of the suitcase, ran off and disappeared like an ink spot into a well of darkness. It happened so fast that Paula just stood frozen by the front of the car, her eyes unblinking pools of disbelief.

"Paula, what the hell kind of neighborhood do you live in that allows their dogs to roam free in the streets, especially vicious dogs?"

Paula shrugged. "I've never seen a black dog like that in this neighborhood, and I know the other dog owners around here because I take Barkly walking every day."

Just then, Jackie popped her head outside of the door of the house, "Girls, come inside. It's getting cold, and I've got dinner waiting!" This snapped Paula and Sam out of their stunned mood.

Paula grabbed Sam's suitcase, seeing she was still shaken up by the weird encounter. "Come on, let's get inside!" Paula patted Sam's back, gently nudging her to the door to shake her friend's troubled mood.

Jackie greeted Sam at the door. "Now what's my long-lost daughter been up all these months? I haven't seen you in ages. You look tired, honey! Paula show Sam to her room."

Sam could only get out "You look great, Jackie!" before being pushed down the hallway to the awaiting guest room. "Love you!" Sam enthused over her shoulder as she was good-naturedly pushed inside the doorway and into the awaiting room by Paula.

Inside was a small but cozy room containing a full bed with down comforter, a mirrored sliding door closet, a small window above a large oak dresser with several high school photos of Sam, Paula, and their friends, and all of Paula's HS trophies from past achievements such as swimming/diving meets sitting on top. "Well, we now know what the inside of a time capsule from 1987 looks like!" Sam joked while looking around the room.

"Ha! Ha! Very funny! Don't be jealous just because I was the better jock in high school!"

Sam went to open the closet to put away her bemouth designer suitcase when Paula stopped her.

"Don't open that! It's crammed with my clothes from when I moved from my place. I'll put this in the master bedroom's walk-in closet. I may barely be able to squeeze in this traveling circus case."

Sam laughed. "Don't open it and let out the flying monkeys or we are all done for!" Sam paused, adding, "Hey, are you sure you don't want me to take the couch? I hate to make you move in with your mom and disturb her sleep with your snoring."

Paula snorted. "Nobody can top my mom's snores, so thanks, but we don't need your fake pity! You can sleep like a queen in my room." Paula wheeled the large suitcase out of the room and down the hall to the master bedroom, saying, "Hurry up, Queen Samantha! My mom will throw us both outside to sleep in the cold if we mess up her dinner!"

When Sam and Paula joined Jackie in the kitchen, the delicious smells of Jackie's home-cooked dinner instantly created a feeling of comfort, and the warmth of the room filled with these two ladies took Samantha back to simpler days.

"Sam, come sit down and enjoy some soup."

Sam's eyes lit up seeing the huge chunks of chicken and thick noodles swimming in the broth. "Jackie, you don't know how much I miss your homemade soups. I've tried to make it myself but just can't get the same taste as yours. And look at this feast!" The crocheted-lace linen tablecloth was set with fine china plates and had a smorgasbord of delicious homemade items such as shepherds' bread, regional cheeses, and huge breaded crab cakes with garlic-butter dipping sauce.

Jackie beamed with pride. "Okay, ladies, I know you're hungry but don't dig in yet. Paula, please say grace."

Paula grabbed Sam's and Jackie's hands. "Dear Lord, bless this meal and the hands that prepared it. And thank you for bringing my bestie, Sammy, here safely from California."

"And thank you, dear Lord, for blessing me with such great hosts as the Johnson family," Sam enthusiastically added.

"Amen to that," Jackie said. "Now please EAT!"

As they ate and chatted, Samantha realized Barkly was missing. "Hey, where's Barkly?"

Paula looked at the clock and started dialing her cell phone. "Our neighbor has kids that adore Barkly, so since I had to pick you up, they took him for his evening walk, but I'll go get him now that we're all here."

As Paula headed out the door, Jackie turned to Sam. "I'm so happy you're here now. I hope you're going to relax and have fun, and not allow anything to trouble you."

Sam put her hand on Jackie's shoulder. "Don't worry, that's all behind me now." Just then Barkly came barreling in the door, greeting Jackie and charging around the table to Sam, who had gotten up, holding her arms out to embrace him. Suddenly Barkly stopped in his tracks, and the hair raised on his back as he started growling.

"Stop that Barkly! You know Sam. It's not been that long," Paula scolded. Barkly's head lowered, and his stance was low as if to pounce, as he backed Sam into the corner of the kitchen.

"Paula!" Sam shrieked.

Paula quickly grabbed Barkly's collar, dragging him around to her side of the table, making him lie down while putting his leash on just in case.

Sam sat down slowly, in disbelief, watching Barkly carefully. Barkly's eyes darted back and forth spastically, looking just above Sam's right shoulder as if he were tracking a fast-moving object.

"Look at Barkly's eyes!" Jackie exclaimed. Everyone gazed at the big German shepherd as his eyes ping-ponged back and forth , never removing their laser focus from the area above Samantha's right shoulder. Sam looked behind her, but there was nothing there that anyone could see except for Barkly.

After an uncomfortable silence, Sam excused herself from the table rather abruptly. "It's been a long day. I'm going to bed." Paula and Jackie both agreed, nodding their heads in unison.

"Yes, honey, please just sleep in as long as you want. We have nothing special planned tomorrow," Jackie said.

Paula offered, "Just let us know if you need anything," as Sam quickly walked down the hallway to her room, closing the door before Paula could finish.

Later that night Paula had a dream that she was on a high cliff overlooking a large body of water like a lake. The water was dark blue and turbulent, with a storm whipping up the waves. Just below, she could see Sam struggling to keep her head above the water. Paula also saw on the shore just below her a dark figure that seemed to be moving closer to Sam. Paula called out to Sam, but she couldn't hear her as her head kept bobbing below the surface of the dark waters. Paula tried to move but was frozen, watching the dark apparition getting closer, cutting a wake through the water towards Sam. The next instant, Paula was diving off the cliff into the waters, but when she bobbed back up to the surface, Sam was nowhere to be found, and instead Paula felt a cold darkness descending upon her, pushing her deeper into the water. She struggled to get to the surface, using her long, athletic legs to kick towards the top, but the more she struggled, the more she seemed to be getting sucked down into a black pit.

Paula woke up with a start, drenched in sweat. Her temporary relief at realizing her near-death encounter was just a nightmare soon evaporated at the sound of tapping fingers on her headboard, that drumming sound, like an impatient staccato that fingers make when someone is waiting for time to pass. She sharply drew in her breath, looking over at Jackie peacefully slumbering, wondering if she was still perhaps in that dream state. But those fingers kept drumming away. Paula shook her mother awake. "Mom! Mom! Do you hear that?" she whispered.

Jackie swatted away her daughter's hand and groggily muttered, "What's wrong?" as the drumming stopped.

Paula explained her dream to Jackie and the weird waking in the morning that definitely wasn't a dream. Instead of scoffing or dismissing the story, Jackie contemplated her daughter's worried face. "I wouldn't mention this just yet to Sam, she's already in such a state. But I have a suggestion, which might help shed some light on this. Take her to Tany! She could probably pick up on what's going on."

Paula frowned in doubt. "The psychic? I don't know, Mom..."

"What do you have to lose? She might be able to pick up on something during a reading or give some clue as to how to shake Sam's shadow."

"But doesn't she charge an arm and leg for her readings?"

Jackie laughed. "If you're looking for money, just ask. My treat!"

Paula got out of bed and dressed in a hurry, grabbed a hundred-dollar bill out of her mom's purse, kissed her head, and swept out the door.

Sam was already up having coffee, with Barkly snoozing nearby. "Wakey wakey eggs and bacy!" Sam chanted.

Paula smiled, trying to hide her worry. "I see you and Barkly are friends again."

"I couldn't sleep so got up early and took him for a walk. It's a lovely neighborhood here in Mystic! What's on the agenda for today?"

Paula grabbed her coat. "You'll see! I have some surprises planned for you today if I can arrange it, so let's get started."

Sam looked suspiciously at Paula. "You know I hate surprises."

Me too, Paula thought as she tried to put the memory of her dream out of her mind. "Well, nothing is that surprising in this town. I think you'll be safe."

They headed out the door and drove off to start their sightseeing. Paula wanted to distract Sam while she called Tany to hopefully set up a visit for that day. She didn't want another night to pass as she recalled with dread the escalating events that Sam had encountered.

Chapter 3

SWORDS

PAULA DROVE STRAIGHT TO THE MYSTIC DINER & RESTAURANT for break-fast where, after ordering eggs benedict and cappuccinos, Paula was able to excuse herself to the restroom to make a frantic call to Tany, begging her to squeeze in a reading for Sam later the same day. Luckily Tany had a last-minute cancellation. Paula let out a long sigh, emerging from the restroom stall and heading back to the colorful blue-and-yel-low booth where Sam sat sipping from her frothy steaming mug. Just as Paula sat down, the plates of food arrived. "Don't you love it when you emerge from the restroom and your food is waiting for you?" Paula said, smiling down at the golden, gleaming hollandaise-drenched eggs and English muffins.

"You were gone long enough. What are you up to?" Sam smiled sus-piciously as she took a bite of bacon.

Paula cleared her throat. "That's for me to know, and you to find out."

After finishing their meal and fighting over the check, Paula shut-tled Sam out the door, and they spent some time nearby window shop-ping. But all Paula could think of was getting to the psychic's place. Sam noticed Paula kept checking her watch. "What, am I boring you with all the tourist shopping for tchotchkes? Do you have some more import-ant place to be?"

"No, but WE do." Paula said while grabbing Sam's hand, navigating her out of the store and into the awaiting car.

As they drove past the historic Elm Grove Cemetery, an expansive, extremely well-kept plot of land where early Mystic sea captains and their families were buried, Paula found herself holding her breath.

Sam chuckled. "And I thought I was the superstitious one! Please breathe, Paula. I don't want you passing out until later tonight at the bar."

Paula sneered at her friend, while her clammy hands held a death grip on the steering wheel. There was no denying the tension emanating off Paula like an Alabama heat wave.

"What the hell is going—?"

"We're HERE!" Paula announced, coming to a sharp stop in front of a white-picket-fenced home. Sam looked quizzically at her friend, one eyebrow raised in doubt. Paula shrugged with a tight-lipped smile and deftly slid out of the car, avoiding any direct gaze.

Paula strode up to the front door while Sam tentatively followed, navigating the fragrant rose garden that encircled the home like a protective Sleeping Beauty moat. Paula knocked firmly, and a petite woman with long flaxen blonde hair, highlighted with streaks of sparkling gray, opened the door with a warm smile. "You must be Paula and Samantha! Please come in." She motioned for them to enter the small foyer. Sam instantly felt at ease as she looked around at the sunlight-dappled room that smelled of flowers, reminding her of the Casablanca lilies she used in her wedding bouquet. "Would either of you like a cup of tea? I have Moroccan mint, chamomile, or Earl Grey if you want something a little stronger."

Sam and Paula were so mesmerized by the sound of windchimes hanging just outside an open window, being played with by a gentle New England breeze, that they both seemed dumbfounded, unable to reply as the sights and sounds held them in a momentary stupor. "Oh, that sounds lovely…" Sam managed, feeling like her mouth was full of honey, wondering if she was just stating how the chimes sounded in her ears or accepting the invitation for tea. "I'd love the mint tea."

Paula, not much of a tea drinker, just shook her head, trying to communicate her polite decline.

"Please sit in the reading room while I get the tea ready." Tany motioned to a quaint sunroom just to the right of the foyer as she spun around on her heels, heading to the kitchen. "Make yourselves at home, I'll be there in a moment."

Sam and Paula headed to the brightly lit, airy room through an arched door where a satin curtain hung, tied with a sash to the side as a partial closure to the room. They sat down at a glass tabletop attached to an ornately carved cherry wood stand, with roses, leaves, and butterfly motifs swirling to the top as if waiting to explode through their glass ceiling. Large windows looked out on the rose garden, giving beautiful yet private views, as more wind chimes clanged in gentle rhythm outside. A painting of a Hawaiian waterfall surrounded by lush tropical flowers was mounted opposite the windows. Sunlight danced across the painting, bouncing off crystals placed on the windowsill as an indoor fountain babbled nearby, giving one the impression that the waterfall was in sparkling movement.

Sam turned to Paula and whispered, "What are we doing here?"

Paula relaxed back into the comfortable wooden chair, resting her slender arms on the chairs, neatly folding her hands in front of her body. "Enjoying the ambiance," she said with a wink.

Sam rolled her eyes and focused on the large crystal pitcher of water in the center of the table. It was filled on the bottom with a rainbow of glitter, small opaline stones, small golden stars, and other little shiny objects she couldn't quite make out. There was also a purple satin sachet, cinched at the top with long tassel closures, and a palm-sized deck of cards. Just then Sam snapped out of her lullaby feeling. "Paula! Did you hijack me for a psychic reading?"

Paula's relaxed stance immediately changed as she sat up straight in her chair. "Well, we are exploring Mystic, after all! What did you think? I was going to bring you to some boring museum?"

Before Sam could say anything, Tany flowed into the sunroom and set the tea in front of Sam, who marveled at the exquisitely thin white china cup accented with a royal-blue diamond pattern. "Here you are, my dear. Oh, I guess I should introduce myself; I'm Tany Tayler, Mystic's most notable psychic if I do say so myself," Tany said with a wink, extending an elegantly long-fingered hand to Sam.

"I'm Sam," was all that Sam could muster.

Paula piped up. "You know my mom, Jackie."

"Oh yes, Paula, she talks about you often, and I must say you are the spitting image of her, in her younger days of course."

Sam took a sip of the tea, trying to calm the butterflies in her stomach, thinking of how she would read Paula the riot act as soon as she could figure out how to escape this little room.

As if reading her mind, Tany took Sam's hands in her own, which were surprisingly warm and strong. "I know you are probably thinking you'd like to kick Paula, but I promise I'm only here for good, and if you truly don't want to receive a reading, I would never force you."

Sam looked into Tany's kind eyes and suddenly felt a calm wash over her. "Yes, of course. I'm just a little shocked, but then my best friend Paula is always full of surprises."

Paula pretended to look around the room playfully, then rested her eyes squarely on Sam with a sheepish grin.

"Okay, then let's begin." Tany started saging the room and lit a tall white candle that smelled of vanilla. She pulled out some crystals from the purple sachet, placing them on four points of the table. Tany closed her eyes and started saying a small prayer.

Sam interrupted, "Don't you need to ask me a question first?"

Tany smiled knowingly. "I only ask the Holy Spirit to guide me and receive those messages by faith like a vessel." Tany picked up a long glass mixing stick, placed it in the glass vase in the middle of the table, and started stirring the water. As she stirred, the glittering treasures whipped into a dazzling frenzy. Tany's crystal-blue eyes darkened to cobalt as she sat stirring, staring intently into the watery vortex.

Sam sat mesmerized, looking at the spinning, glittering water, while comforting vanilla tickled her nose at the same time the babbling fountain whispered in her ears. Her mind flowered open, bathed in this sensory bath.

"I see you have lived a good life and have gained good karma from past lives. But I see darkness clouding your life recently, blocking your psyche and making you feel empty inside, like an avatar of your former self." Tany kept spinning her wand in the kaleidoscope pitcher while talking to Sam. "I see two shadows, one is pure of heart, innocent, almost a memory. It is tied to you, an intrinsic part of your soul. But it is being overshadowed by the other. This larger shadow is wicked, feeding off this small shadow that you have created."

Sam sat entranced in silence.

Tany suddenly stopped spinning the water, grabbed the tarot deck and firmly shuffled the cards, making crisp clicking sounds as the cards glided past one another. She placed the shuffled pile in front of Sam. "Please cut the deck into three piles, then place them back together in any order you wish."

Sam obeyed, moving sections of the cards into three neat piles, then organizing them back, taking the left pile onto the right and top-ping it off onto the middle deck. Tany took the cards into her elegant hands and placed four cards facedown in front of Sam, flipping them over one at a time slowly. The first card had an image of a huge tow-er being struck by lightning at the top, while a man and woman fell from its heights. The second card was the Three of Swords: a huge red heart filled the image with three swords piercing through it as raining clouds surrounded. The third card was titled The Moon, containing an image of a huge Sun with an eclipsing half-moon, flanked by two tow-ers and two dogs peering up at it while a lobster crawled out of the water in the foreground. The last card with the Roman number XIII at the top was Death, armored in black like a dark knight riding a white spirit steed and holding the death banner. A king lay on the ground, his crown toppled, while a small child and woman kneeled before the red-eyed horse. Nearby a holy man with a pope-like headdress seemed to be pleading with Death to no avail as the sun set between two towers in the background.

Tany's eyes narrowed as she nodded, as if expecting this card. "You suffered a great shock, a huge loss, recently. The Tower card is one of unexpected shock that can throw you into chaos, so seemingly solid things you took for granted were brought into question, making you feel like the rug was pulled out from under you. This Tower experience and loss brought you deep grief, piercing you to your very core. This sorrowful loss you pushed down deep into your subconscious, where the Moon exposes your shadow self, things you are hiding not only from others but yourself." Tany tapped on the last card. "Death comes for all, the powerful, the weak, the old, the young, women, children, it has no discretion and can't be bargained with." Tany continued as Sam's face slackened with recognition. "This shocking loss that caused you so much pain, that you chose to hide, drew a dark entity to you." Tany looked troubled. "Did you lose a child?"

Suddenly Sam's body shook uncontrollably as she tried to fight back the tears welling in her eyes, to no avail, as slick tracks glided down her face.

"Oh, Sam," Paula whispered, taking her hand in hers.

Sam started sobbing, and through tears, managed to muster, "Yes, I lost my beautiful baby girl, just weeks before she was to be born. It was Derek's and my first, and I couldn't imagine what I did to deserve such a tragedy. I blamed myself, the doctors that couldn't save her, and even God. I just couldn't deal with the emptiness that occupied the space inside of me that formerly nurtured her, so I instead nurtured my grief, deep inside myself, putting on a brave face for my friends and family, and dove back into work to escape the scrutiny of others and my own mind."

Tany nodded in sympathy. "The cards confirmed what I saw in the watery messages. The young innocent shadow is not your daughter, who has passed on immediately to the afterlife as a pure, higher-vibrational soul, but the sorrow you are nursing over her loss. This deep, untapped darkness inside you was like a beacon to the shadow entity that preyed on you, feeding off that shadowy part of yourself, further emboldened by your fears."

Sam shoulders shivered in self-realization.

"You can see the two towers repeating in several of the tarot cards, representing these two entities, one of your making and one of the devil's offspring. You need to realize that in death there is also transformation. The setting sun can also be a rising one, bringing transformation, closure, and eventual regeneration. Nobody knows God's plans, but we must strive forward not with vision of the exact path but blindly in faith that God's mysterious plans will eventually be known to us, if not in this lifetime, then in the beyond."

Tany's words rained down on Sam's heart, opening a space that had been closed for a long while. She felt comforted more than she had in years.

"You must get rid of this entity. It has attached itself to you and will not leave willingly. It is important to fight both shadows and seek to heal that part of yourself, bringing to light what was hidden, but that will take time. Right now you need to clear the space for that healing to happen. And that means getting rid of this tagalong, poor excuse for a poltergeist."

Sam smiled a bit as Paula squeezed her hand even tighter.

"But how do we do that?" Paula implored.

Tany leaned forward as she gazed at the pitcher of water. "I believe this shadow has attached itself not directly to Sam, as she's protected by her angels, including her departed daughter, and God, but to something Sam has in her possession. So it uses whatever that item is as a home base from which it can literally haunt and harass Sam."

Just then Paula's phone rang, startling all three women. "I'm so sorry, I thought I had it on vibrate. It's my mom. I'll just call her back la—"

"No!" Tany firmly interrupted. "Take the call. I have a feeling it's tied into this."

Paula answered the phone. "Mom, yes, we're at Tany's... Mom, I can barely hear you over all the barking. What? Okay, I see. I'll be right there." Paula looked at Tany in disbelief.

"Well, what did your mom say?" Sam impatiently asked.

"She needs us to come back and deal with Barkly. I guess ever since we left, he's been clawing and barking incessantly at her closet door. And when she threw him out of the room, locking the door, he kept pacing and whining in front of her bedroom. And when she tired of that and chained him outside, he started howling, so she had to bring him back in, and he started up with the barking. I have to get home and see what..." Paula's eyes lit up with realization.

"Sam, it's your luggage!"

"What's my luggage got to do with—"

"Sam, remember how that dog came out of nowhere when you took your bag from the car? And didn't you say you went to that hotel in San Francisco where you first started to get all those creepy feelings?"

Sam sharply drew a breath in as if punched in the gut. "Yes, you're right, I did use that same luggage! It's the one I always travel with for business or even personal."

Tany nodded. "That fits the bill. If you were alone, feeling sorrowful in your room, a dark entity residing there could easily have been drawn to you and attached itself to your main possession."

Paula burst into action, pulling Sam out of her chair and slapping the hundred-dollar bill on the table, as she rushed out of the room. "Thanks a bunch, Tany! Sorry to break up the reading, but I gotta get home to my mom right NOW!"

Sam tried to keep up with Paula's long legs, sprinting to the car, and they opened the doors to get in.

Tany shouted from the doorway, "Wait! You need to hear how to completely neutralize the shadow!" Tany was met with the sound of slamming car doors and kicked-up gravel as the Subaru sped off down the lane.

Chapter 4

DEATH.

WHEN PAULA PULLED UP TO THE HOUSE, it was already dusk. "Wait here! Don't you move a muscle!"

"But, Paula, please let me help." Her friend's glare made Sam sink deeply into her seat, defeated.

Paula flung the front door open, where she found Jackie in frustrated tears. "Would you please quiet that damn dog of yours! He's giving me a nervous breakdown!"

"Don't worry, Mom! He probably just saved Sam's life, if not both of ours."

Jackie gave her daughter a look as if she had lost her mind and continued clapping her hands over her ears, shaking her head.

Paula grabbed Barkly's collar. "Good boy!" Barkly barely looked at her, whining shortly in greeting and then barking furiously at the door, trying to scratch his way under the gap in the door and wood flooring. "It's okay, boy. I'm going to take it from here." Paula opened the door, almost toppled over by Barkly rushing to the closet door and growling. Paula suddenly felt a tug of fear as she opened the closet door. There sat the unassuming black roller bag, but she could feel tangible energy as she grabbed it, shoving it down the hall and out the front door as Barkly tried to bite at the sides and wheels.

Jackie looked bewildered as she yelled out, "I thought Sam was planning to stay longer?"

"Mom, I'll explain later, just keep Barkly inside!"

Sam watched as her friend tossed the huge suitcase into the car. Neither said a word as they tore off down the road towards the harbor.

Sam whispered, "Where are you going?"

Paula put her finger up to her lips to hush Sam as they drove off in silence into the darkening nightfall. When Paula reached the bridge heading over the harbor entrance, she pulled over to the side of the road and motioned to Sam to get out of the car. Pulling Sam by the elbow away from the car, Paula wheeled around, saying, "Quick! Grab all the heavy stones you can. I'm going to fill that damned suitcase of yours with rocks and toss it into the Atlantic Ocean!"

"Have you lost your mind? That's Louis Vuitton luggage! Do you know how much that cost me?"

"No, Sam, it's the only way! I'll buy you another bag, but this one is going to the bottom of the bay!" After grabbing all the heavy rocks they could, Paula opened the tailgate, unzipped the black bag, pulling out all of Sam's clothing and personal items, then stacking rocks inside. When filled, Paula tried to push the roller case up the sidewalk onto the bridge, but it was so heavy, Sam had to push from behind as Paula pulled. The wheels shrieked and groaned, which sounded more like a personal protest than just the physical weight of the case.

"Push harder!" Paula demanded.

"I'm giving it all I can! It's so dark out here, I can barely see where I'm pushing it to."

When they crested the top of the bridge, Paula grabbed the front of the case and pushed it out between a gap in the short side railing. As the suitcase tipped forward, Sam realized too late that a piece of her clothing had got caught in the suitcase zipper. She felt herself falling, like the woman from the Tower tarot card, in slow motion. She hit the cold water hard, knocking the wind out her lungs as she hit the case first, which was sinking quickly into the dark abyss.

From the bridge above, Paula watched as a feeling of nausea over-took her, flooding her mind with déjà vu images from her dream earlier that day. She couldn't see Sam anymore and with the current pulling the water out to the ocean in the darkness, it might mean her own life if she jumped in after Sam. Paula only hesitated enough to take a deep breath and dove into the water below. She couldn't see Sam, but some-how, she knew she was closing in, like a homing message being re-ceived from a source beyond. All those years of diving and swim meets helped to propel her downward. She felt Sam's head and limp body and tried to force her loose, but she couldn't seem to tear her free of the black bag. Mustering a reserve strength she didn't know she had, Paula tore Sam free from the blackness and swam as hard as she could for the surface, breaching with a burst of choked air.

Swimming to shore, Paula pulled Sam out and started preforming CPR. "Come on, Sam! Fight for it!" as Paula physically tried to pump life back into her limp friend. Paula stopped as Sam spit up water, choking and gasping for air. "Thank you, Jesus!" Paula cried as Sam sputtered for air. Paula helped her friend up as she patted her back hard.

"Okay! Okay! That's enough!" Sam managed, her body shaking and shivering from the near-death experience.

Both women shuffled back to the car, letting a huge sigh out as they flopped into the seats. After silently watching a few stray harbor boats coming in, Sam looked over at Paula. "I just want to thank you, Paula, for saving my life. Although it was your crazy idea that got me into this mess in the first place, I couldn't ask for a better friend."

Paula looked fondly at Sam. "You know you're my best friend and that I'd do anything for you. Even if it means putting my own life on the line. I just hope that this takes care of that evil spirit and that you can heal fully."

Sam nodded in agreement and reached over to squeeze Paula's hand.

"I feel like perhaps I'm making up for not realizing how grief-stricken you were when you lost Chelsea. You just sort of went quiet on me, then appeared to bounce right back to your usual self. I felt something was 'off,' but I just didn't know how to broach the subject with you. I'm sorry for that." Paula's voice trailed off.

Tears rolled down Sam's face as she patted her friend's hand. "Listen, Paula, you are and were for me always a rock. There is nothing anyone could have said or done to change it. I had to go through my own grieving process in my way. I still am coming out the other side. And now for the first time, opening up a bit more like this, I think I can come to a better place. I won't ever be whole, but I'll be a whole lot better with a friend like you by my side."

Paula smiled. "Let's get you back home and dried off. Lucy, we got a lot of 'splaining to do!"

Sam chucked. "Yes, your mom will get an earful, but at least it won't be from Barkly's howling anymore! I owe that dog of yours a debt of gratitude too!"

"Lucky for you he'll take it in belly rubs!" Paula winked as they drove back home. Sam closed her eyes and let the motion of the warm car rock her into a peaceful place she hadn't felt in years.

Epilogue

{Five years later in Florida. Two Cuban Americans
down by the beach speaking in Spanish.}

"**HEY, JUAN, YOU KNOW THAT RING** I found last week washed up on the beach? Turned out it was worth a fortune! Too bad you weren't with me that day or I would've split the money with you."

Juan rolled his eyes. "Abuelito, you always try to rub it in when I don't go out with you trolling the beachfront for treasures."

"I know you think you're getting too big for helping this old man. Just wanting to chase the girls now that you're sixteen instead of helping your old Papi Carlos!"

Juan shook his head no, smiling at his grandfather.

"Hey, look over there!" Both their eyes turned to a dark object covered in seaweed. They strode over to the pile, flipping off the pieces of beach wood and sand half burying the object. "Well, look at that! It's a piece of luggage, and a nice designer one at that! Quick, I'll get the pickup, and we can load it into the truck."

Juan continued digging the black luggage out of its sand tomb as Carlos backed up the truck onto the beach.

"Juan, hurry up and load it! It's starting to get lighter out, and I don't want to get caught by the beach patrol!"

"But it's super heavy, Abuelo!"

"Come on! When I was your age, I could lift a VW Bug! Put your back into it!"

Juan, not to be outdone by Carlos, heaved the bag out of the sand and got the front tipped onto the tailgate.

"Come on, slowpoke!"

Juan tried but couldn't lift it all the way. "I'm telling you, it's too heavy! Let's open it up and see if it's even worth taking."

"No time for that, we can sort through the contents safer outside of any prying eyes. Just push it into the bed and stop complaining!"

Juan finally got enough leverage to tip most of the case onto the truck, sliding it across the grooved floor bed until it was up against the cab.

Jumping down from the tailgate, he grabbed a Coke out of the mini-cooler in the truck bed and sat down for a second to catch his breath, taking a few sips of the slightly bittersweet drink. Climbing into the cab, Juan kicked off his flip-flops, sticking one foot out the rolled-down window.

"Well, it's about time Your Highness gets his ass in the car!" Carlos chuckled.

"Abuelo, don't be so impatient! I heard you drumming your fingers on the back window of the car while I was taking a breather."

"What do you mean, mijo?" Carlos looked confused.

"Oh, now there is no hurry, eh?" Juan laughed. "I heard you drumming your fingers impatiently!"

"I swear, mijo, I didn't do that!"

Juan huffed, crossing his other foot over the first, both sandy feet now sticking out the window. "Never mind, Papi. let's see what good fortune is in store for us now that we've found such a treasure!"

The End...?

www.ingramcontent.com/pod-product-compliance
Lightning Source LLC
Chambersburg PA
CBHW070653130626
46555CB00006B/2856